A catalogue record for this book is available from the British Library

Adapted from the television script by Keith Littler, based on the original stories by Colin Reader.
Photographs by James Lampard.

Published by Ladybird Books Ltd.
80 Strand London WC2R 0RL
A Penguin Company

7 9 10 8 6

ISBN-13: 978-1-84422-564-4
ISBN-10: 1-8442-2564-x

Printed in China

The Detectives

"Toot! Toot!" Little Red Tractor welcomed
Ryan and Amy as they walked into
the yard.

"Hello, you two. Why the long faces?"
Stan asked.

"We have to do a project on the
countryside," Ryan said. He didn't want
to do school work at the weekend.

"Whenever I have to do a job I don't like, I always try to find a way to make it fun," said Stan. "So whoever gets the most questions right, gets one of my homemade buns."

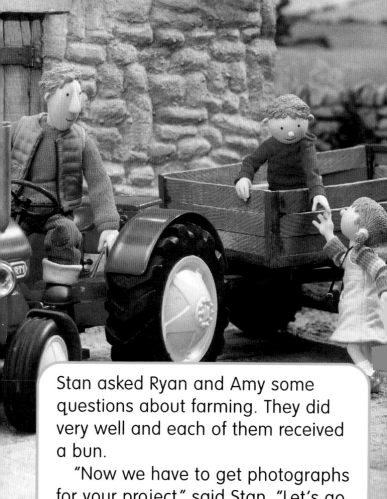

Stan asked Ryan and Amy some questions about farming. They did very well and each of them received a bun.

"Now we have to get photographs for your project," said Stan. "Let's go and see Mr Jones to get a picture of another farmer."

They found Mr Jones looking at a wellington boot brochure. He was trying to decide which colour to buy. Then he told them that Big Blue had a scratch from an accident earlier that day.

Of course, Stan, Ryan and Amy wanted to know all about it.

Mr Jones told his side of the story.

"I was driving along, you see, carefully watching the road like a good driver should. From out of nowhere comes Walter, singing away, not paying attention to the road. And then in screeches Stumpy, out of control."

According to Mr Jones, he stopped just in time to prevent a crash, but Stumpy went flying over his handlebars and onto the grass.

"If it wasn't for my quick thinking… it could have been very nasty," said Mr Jones.

The children took their photo of Mr Jones with Big Blue. Then, with Stan and Little Red Tractor, they went off to Beech Garage. They found Walter in the shop, getting some toffees.

"Hi, Walter! Are you okay after the accident?" called Stan.

"Fine," replied Walter, looking uncomfortable. "I was driving along looking at the road, when from out of nowhere comes Mr Jones. He had something over his face. Then Stumpy appeared, all over the place. I had to think fast…"

According to Walter, he just managed to prevent a crash, but Stumpy went flying over his handlebars. "It could have been nasty," said Walter.

"Hmm, well that's slightly different to how Mr Jones remembers it," said Stan thoughtfully.

Just then, Stumpy roared up on Nipper.

"We heard about the accident," said Stan.

"Oh yes, that was a close one," replied Stumpy. "Lucky I acted so quickly."

"**You** acted so quickly?" asked Stan.

"Yes, I was driving along very carefully, when from out of nowhere comes Mr Jones, reading a paper. Then Walter suddenly appears, singing along to the radio. Fortunately, I made everyone stop in time. It could have been nasty," he said. "I just wish I could find my hat," he added.

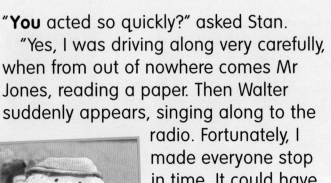

Stan promised to look for Stumpy's hat. "We have to go and look for a few things for Ryan and Amy's school project," he explained.

"Toot! Toot!" Little Red Tractor was ready to go.

They soon reached the T-junction.

"Hmm, something doesn't seem right," said Stan. "Look at the marks on the road. That only happens when you put the brakes on really hard."

There were definitely three sets of marks!

"It looks like they all had to brake really hard at the same time," said Amy.

"Now, if we can work out which of these tracks was left by Nipper, we can start looking for Stumpy's hat," said Stan.

It didn't take the detectives very long to work out that the smallest tracks belonged to Nipper. Stumpy must have flown over the gate!

There was no sign of the hat, but Stan noticed something else… hoofprints!

These hoofprints belonged to Veronica the cow.

"Let's follow them," cried Ryan.

The detectives followed the prints until they found… a sheep!

They took a photograph for their project and carried on their search.

Finally they found Veronica,
wearing Stumpy's hat!
It was time to go back to Beech
Garage and find out the true story.

At Beech Garage, Little Red Tractor, Stan and the children found Mr Jones holding a blue wellington boot. As he couldn't make up his mind, he had bought all the colours!

"Did you find my hat?" Stumpy asked the newcomers.

"Well, we went to the accident site," Stan said.

"We had to do some detective work and follow the clues," added Amy and Ryan.

"The funny thing is, the clues don't match up with the stories you all told," Stan told Walter, Stumpy and Mr Jones.

The three drivers shuffled their feet and looked embarrassed. The true story was about to come out!

"Mr Jones was driving down the road, trying to read a magazine," said Stan.

"And Walter drives in, singing along to the radio and not looking where he's going," added Ryan and Amy.

"Then Stumpy drives in on Nipper, completely out of control, and all three reach the T-junction at the same time," chorused the detectives. "Luckily everyone managed to stop."

"You all should have been driving a lot more carefully," said Stan.

Walter, Mr Jones and Stumpy looked very guilty. They said sorry to the detectives.

"I don't suppose," added Stumpy, "that you managed to find my hat?"

Stan remembered the children's farm project. There was time for one last question. "Here's a good one," he said. "What do you think the most important piece of equipment is to a farmer?"

"Beats me," replied Walter.
"Is it wellington boots?" asked Mr Jones.
"Is it his hat?" beamed Stumpy.
Ryan and Amy knew the answer. "His tractor!"

Stan grinned. He was thinking of one tractor in particular.

"Toot! Toot!" prompted Little Red Tractor.

Everybody laughed in agreement!

ILLUSTRATIONS

Cover and half-title page: Borg. Lat. 183 fol. 34 v; frontispiece: Vat. Lat. 3467 fol. 176 v; p. 7: Barb. Lat. 614 fol. 219 v; p. 9: Reg. Lat. 124 fol. 35 v; p. 10: Vat. Lat. 3769 fol. 56 v; p. 13: Borg. Lat. 183 fol. 34 v; p. 14: Barb. Lat. 381 fol. 34 r; p. 17: Rossiano 119 fol. 55 r; p. 18: Barb. Lat. 585 CCXI v; p. 21: Barb. Lat. 585 fol. 7 r; p. 22: Chigi C VII 205 fol. 158 r; p. 25: Rossiano 119 fol. 60 r; p. 26: Barb. Lat. 610 fol. 184 v; p. 28: Vat. Lat. 20 fol. 3 v; p. 29: Vat. Lat. 17 fol. 3 v; p. 30: Barb. Lat. 425 fol. 38 v; p. 32: Borg. Lat. III 8 fol. 166 v; p. 33: Vat. Lat. 973 fol. 19 r; p. 34: Urb. Lat. 110 fol. 104 v; p. 37: Chigi C VIII 230 fol. 14 v; p. 38: Rossiano 204 fol. 10 r; p. 39: Vat. Lat. 83 fol. 206 v; p. 41: Barb. Lat. 382 fol. 198 v; p. 42: Vat. Lat. 39 fol. 65 r; p. 43: Vat. Lat. 1434 fol. 217 r; p. 45: Borg. Lat. 183 fol. 35 r; p. 46: Vat. Lat. 3769 fol. 166 v; p. 49: Vat. Lat. 3769 fol. 117 r; p. 50: Vat. Lat. 39 fol. 171 v; p. 52: Barb. Lat. 610 fol. 223 v; p. 53: Vat. Lat. 1430 fol. 5 r; p. 54: Barb. Lat. 487 fol. 42 r; p. 57: Vat. Lat. 3781 fol. 67 v; p. 58: Reg. Lat. 124 fol. 8 v; p. 59: Reg. Lat. 124 fol. 23 v; p. 61: Vat. Lat. 8700 fol. 122 v; p. 62: Chigi C IV 109 fol. 120 r; p. 65: Vat. Lat. 967 fol. 2 r; p. 66: Vat. Lat. 3769 fol. 118 r; p. 69: Vat. Lat. 3770 fol. 151 v; p. 70: Vat. Lat. 1854 fol. 1 r; p. 72: Rossiano 1164 fol. 126 v; p. 73: Capponi 218 fol. 209 v; p. 74: Reg. Lat. 538 fol. 10 r; p. 76: Vat. Lat. 1388 fol. 2 r; p. 78: Ott. Lat. 584 fol. 121 v. Ornamental illumination on pp. 8, 12, 16, 20, 24, 36, 40, 44, 48, 56, 60, 64, 68, and 76 is from Vat. Lat. 3770 fol. 9 r. Ornamental illumination on pp. 11, 15, 19, 23, 27, 31, 35, 47, 51, 55, 63, 67, 71, 75, and 79 is from Reg. Lat. 538 fol. 10 r.

"Why are you frightened, and why do doubts arise in your hearts? Look at my hands and my feet; see that it is I myself. Touch me and see; for a ghost does not have flesh and bones as you see that I have." And when he had said this, he showed them his hands and his feet.

— LUKE 24:38-40

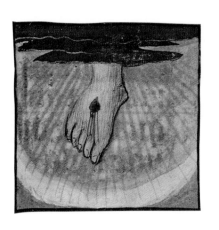

Jesus said..."I am

the resurrection and the life.

Those who believe in me,

even though they die,

will live..."

—JOHN 11:25

The third day He rose again from the dead. He ascended into heaven, and sitteth on the right hand of God the Father Almighty; from thence He shall come to judge the quick and the dead.

—Apostles' Creed

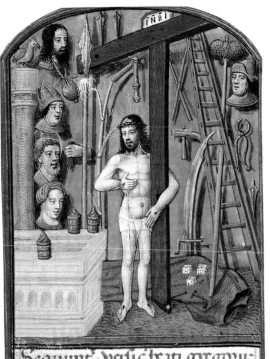

Domine iesu xpe a
dozo te in cruce pede
tem ~ cozona spinea

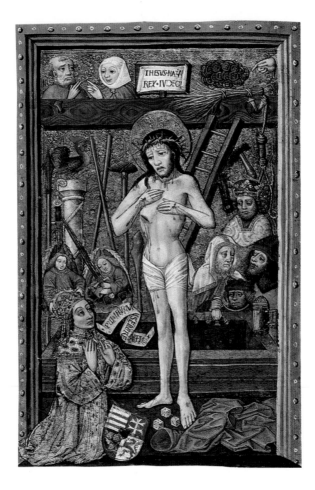

The next day...the chief priests and the Pharisees gathered before Pilate and said, "Sir, we remember what that impostor said while he was still alive, 'After three days I will rise again.'"

—MATTHEW 27:62–63

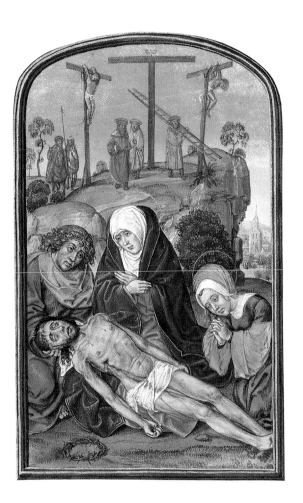

Then Joseph bought a linen
cloth, and taking down
the body, wrapped it in the
linen cloth, and laid it in a
tomb that had been hewn out
of the rock. He then rolled
a stone against the door
of the tomb.

—MARK 15:46

After these things, Joseph of Arimathea, who was a disciple of Jesus...asked Pilate to let him take away the body of Jesus. Pilate gave him permission; so he came and removed his body.

—John 19:38

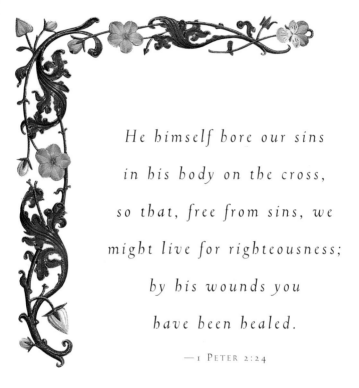

He himself bore our sins

in his body on the cross,

so that, free from sins, we

might live for righteousness;

by his wounds you

have been healed.

—1 PETER 2:24

Then Pilate wondered if he
were already dead; and
summoning the centurion,
he asked him whether he had
been dead for some time.

—MARK 15:44

But when they came to Jesus
and saw that he was already
dead, they did not break
his legs. Instead, one of the
soldiers pierced his side with
a spear, and at once blood
and water came out.

—JOHN 19:33–34

```
SPIRITUSALMEUENISU  DERADIRECTUSABARCE
UTTIBIDEUOTAMMENTE  ETBENECREDULACORDA
TUDEDICESUATISQUIS  ESQUOQUEUITAEQUEM
EXPATREPROMISSUS    NTIAMITTERESEME
PROMISITCHRISTUSA   QUUMLAUDENOUUMQUE
ALTITHRONIDONUMCA   ETPIAPACTIOSPONSAE
INCRUCEQUASPONSUSR  GALISANGUINISOSTRO
DOTAUITDESPONSAUI   SCAMMATESAECLIHOC
CUIDASERGOBENEINT   ECTUSINCULACARPIT
MYSTERIAINTERNEDO   SATQUEOMNIAPENSAT
QUALITERIPSAPATRIS  PIENTIAXPSINORBEM
TEPICNUSDEDERITCO   SPONSAENOBILISARRA
ESSESUAEUOLUITDUM   AUCTORESOMNEMHANC
FORMASTIETMOLETU    PICISINTERIORAET
NONERITULLATIBINI   COSCRUTABERISILLA
NAGCREATURAINUISA   CONSPECTIBUSALMIS

UITTEBISENIMUNSEN   LARESE ATOR IT
CHRISTUSDANSCLARU   ANDATUBINIETAMORIS
UTDEUSEXTOTOCORDI   LLATURHONOREIPSA
ALMUSAMETURAMORQ    TIACUIDETUROMNIS
EXINUTFRATRISCUN    LECTENTURAMOREM
QUODCRUXALMADEIBE   CTOSCEMATESICNAT
NAMPARSSURSUMERE    DEIPIEMANDATAMOREM
TRANSUERSAPACEMDA   AMCUFRATRETENDA
CONSTITUITSANCTA    ATISSUMMUSAMATOR
CRISTUSQUICRUCEER   NEIXUSHOSTIAPACIS
PROPTERAMICORUMPIU  ARBITERORBISAMOREM
DILECTAPONENSANIMA  ATQEXEMPLARELIQUIT
HUNCTUSANCTIPICAN   ALLENDISEMPERAMORE
SPIRITUSINDEMIHI    OMNISNOXIUSABSIT
QUATENUSAUCTACRUC   IUINAECLORIAMECUM
CARMINEPERMANEATTU  PLEBISCARMINEMUTM
OSETRITEPACISCAELE  STEMPSALLERECANTUM
```

ASTSOBOLESDOMINIE · DEVS · DOMINANTIVMVBIQHIC
EXPANSISMANIBVSMOREFORMANTISIHABENDMEN
PERDOCETHVNCVVMIGREXITFICATCOLITATQ
ETSIGMOREFATINGANTHSXIPVENAMSVAMEMBRAHAC
RITEPROBANTPLSETPVENDETQ · PARENTEM
NAMHVNCSCRIPTIONVSTIPITAMENTAMALORVMEST
ETPROBOQVODRECXVAXNATQPOTENTER
QVAEOCCIDITRECELARVPITVAHMAISVXDOGMATACOMPLENS
DRVMMNOSSIPITAHSAIAHMALEGVISQHANC
AETERNVDOMINIE AETOAVCTORSANCTHICOR EST
ORADSVMMICVNLTADELENTQVIASANGVINEDVS
ETSIBRADERIDPITTPRAEDAMPROBASANCTAPROFVNDO
CRVSESTEPOSITVSD E RATDESARCGERS
PRINCIPIDIVMHICDEVSNAMEACFINTSORTGOEST
LVXETPVMAGOPATRISOSSPLENDORGLORIACRISTVS
HOMOVSIONDPATRISOLVERBVMOXLVMINELVPENLVNA
ACQVAMANDOMINISEVVIRTVSDVXQPROPHETAEST
QVEMVNIGENAMIVSTEQEMPRIMIGENAOREFATEMVR
NAZAREVSQVVMOFFENSIOPITACSCANDALINIQVIS
ANGVLVSATQVELAPISCANSVSOHINCIANVAMVNDO
INDVTAENATVRASEIQDOGMATECRIRISTVS
INDICETEXPONALEGAECQVOQVEVESTIS
BISIGNIFICATNAMGERSINGRAMMATERATOR
SVMMIPOTENSAVCTORSNETOMNIARECTOR
ADQVEMMVNDVSPERTANETNSTADACPONTACAETHER
NOSTRACNATVRAHAECIATACCREANTIES
NAMAVCTOREHAECILVQICLAVDITETARVA
OBTESITHVMANOATGLAVDITISVECCEPOTENTEM
IPSETAMENOSTENSVSTOPEREORBHVIC
ANGELVSHVICSFONSISTEETOEVOIOPLEBIST
ATQDOCENSSAPIENCRAPACIETLVSQVOQVECVSTOS
FONSBRACHIVMETPANISDIVINAPETRAMAGISTER
STELLAORIENSQINTCVRAPOTENSINTENTAMEDELA
CLAVISETHICDAVIDLAETAIAETAGNVSHONESTVS
SERPENSSANCTIFICANSINCLVSTRISETVITARAPINA
VERMISHOMOSQETETRAXITBHOSTEETVITARAPINA
MONSAQVILAPARACLITVSSICLEOPASTORETEDVS
FVNDAMENTMOVISSACREDODNSPEVOTASACERDOS
MELCHIPONTIFICISSADEHVINVMQVOQVEPANEMET
QVIVITVLVSARIESCARNEDCVAESSATVSSACRAFINCTVS
VICTIMAPATREDEOSATVSABSQVECADVCO
QVIDAMNASENSITETIGLEQVIOMNIBVSANTEEST
QIASTRAESIDERATOMNIAVELFERVANTE
VIRGINEHICESTNATVSMATREMTEMPORENARTO
ATQVEHOMINEMVTSEARETABRAHICRVCISIVIT
QVIESTSATORATOEINVSXPSDEO

Now when the centurion and those with him, who were keeping watch over Jesus, saw the earthquake and what took place, they were terrified and said, "Truly this man was God's Son!"

—MATTHEW 27:54

When the centurion saw what
had taken place, he praised
God and said, "Certainly
this man was innocent."

—LUKE 23:47

Domine lábia méa
apéries.
Et os méū annū
ciábit láudem tuā.

"*Father, the hour has come;
glorify your Son so that
the Son may glorify you...*"

—JOHN 17:1

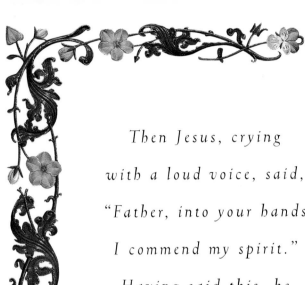

Then Jesus, crying
with a loud voice, said,
"Father, into your hands
I commend my spirit."
Having said this, he
breathed his last.

—LUKE 23:46

And about three o'clock
Jesus cried with a loud voice,
"Eli, Eli, lema sabachthani?"
that is, "My God, my God,
why have you forsaken me?"

—Matthew 27:46

...he humbled himself
and became obedient to
the point of death—even
death on a cross.

—Philippians 2:8

One of the criminals who were hanged there kept deriding him....But the other rebuked him, saying, "Do you not fear God...." Then he said, "Jesus, remember me when you come into your kingdom." He replied, "Truly I tell you, today you will be with me in Paradise."

—LUKE 23:39–43

Those who passed by derided

him, shaking their heads

and saying, "Aha! You who

would destroy the temple

and build it in three days,

save yourself, and come

down from the cross!"

—MARK 15:29–30

And the people stood by,
watching; but the leaders
scoffed at him, saying,
"He saved others;
let him save himself if
he is the Messiah of God,
his chosen one!"

—LUKE 23:35

Meanwhile, standing

near the cross of Jesus

were his mother, and

his mother's sister, Mary

the wife of Clopas,

and Mary Magdalene.

— JOHN 19:25

Then Jesus said,

"Father, forgive them;

for they do not know what

they are doing."

—LUKE 23:34

Onuerte nos de
ns falutaris nr̄.
Et auerte irā.
tuam a nobis Deus i ad

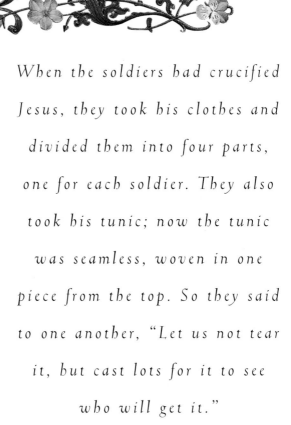

When the soldiers had crucified Jesus, they took his clothes and divided them into four parts, one for each soldier. They also took his tunic; now the tunic was seamless, woven in one piece from the top. So they said to one another, "Let us not tear it, but cast lots for it to see who will get it."

—JOHN 19:23–24

And with him they crucified

two bandits, one on his right

and one on his left.

—MARK 15:27

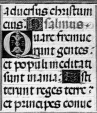

ena secta pars
seculeacd matutini. a
stiterunt
reges terr
ir, et pri
cipes cō
uenerunt in unū ad
uersus dominum, et

Aduersus christum
eius. Psalmus.
Quare fremue
runt gentes
et populi meditati
sunt inania: asti
terunt reges terre
et principes conue

When they came to the place
that is called The Skull,
they crucified Jesus there
with the criminals...

—LUKE 23:33

It was nine o'clock

in the morning when

they crucified him.

—MARK 15:25

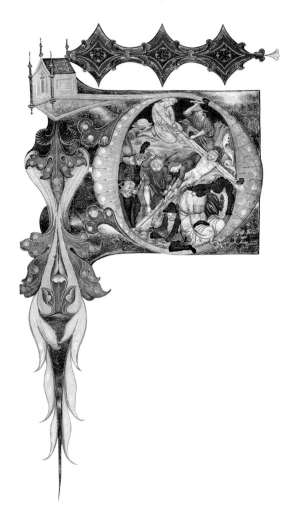

Over his head they
put the charge against
him, which read,
"This is Jesus, the
King of the Jews."

—Matthew 27:37

...carrying the cross
by himself, he went out to
what is called The Place of
the Skull, which in Hebrew
is called Golgotha.

—JOHN 19:17

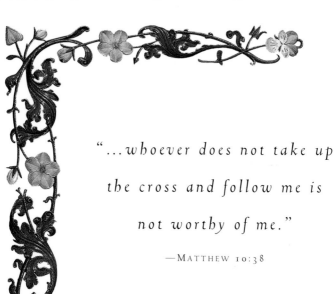

"...whoever does not take up

the cross and follow me is

not worthy of me."

—Matthew 10:38

...and after twisting some
thorns into a crown, they put
it on his head. They put a reed
in his right hand and knelt
before him and mocked him,
saying, "Hail, King of the
Jews!" They spat on him,
and took the reed and
struck him on the head.

—MATTHEW 27:29-30

OROTERAMVSARASVMARESORD

OROTERAMVSARAS ARASVMARESORD

"*His blood be on us and*

on our children!"

—Matthew 27:25

succeeded him, Sixtus added books. By 1455 the library held 1,200 volumes, and a catalogue compiled in 1481 listed 3,500, making it by far the largest collection of books in the Western world.

And The Vatican Library has kept growing: through purchase, commission, donation, and military conquest. Nor did the popes restrict themselves to ecclesiastical subjects. Bibles, theological texts, and commentaries on canon law are here in abundance, to be sure, but so are the Latin and Greek classics that placed The Vatican Library at the very heart of all Renaissance learning. Over the centuries, the library has acquired some of the world's most significant collections of literary works, including the Palatine Library of Heidelberg, the Cerulli collection of Persian and Ethiopian manuscripts, the great Renaissance libraries of the Duke of Urbino and of Queen Christiana of Sweden, and the matchless seventeenth-century collections of the Barberini, the Ottoboni, and Chigi. Today the library contains over one million printed books—including eight thousand published during the first fifty years of the printing press—in addition to 150,000 manuscripts and some 100,000 prints. Assiduously collected and carefully preserved over the course of almost six hundred years, these unique works of art and knowledge, ranging from the secular to the profane, are featured in this ongoing series, Treasures of The Vatican Library, for the delectation of lovers of great books and breathtaking works of art.

Treasures of The Vatican Library: Book Illustration

*T*AKE UP MY CROSS..., the fifth volume in the Treasures of The Vatican Library series, offers a selection of miniature masterworks of book illustration from the collections of one of the world's greatest repositories of classical, medieval, and Renaissance culture. The Vatican Library, for six hundred years celebrated as a center of learning and a monument to the art of the book, is, nevertheless, little known to the general public, for admission to the library traditionally has been restricted to qualified scholars. Since very few outside the scholarly community have ever been privileged to examine the magnificent hand-lettered and illuminated manuscript books in the library's collections, the artwork selected for the series volumes is all the more poignant, fascinating, and appealing.

Of course, the popes had always maintained a library, but in the fifteenth century, Pope Nicholas V decided to build an edifice of unrivaled magnificence to house the papacy's growing collections—to serve the entire "court of Rome," the clerics and scholars associated with the papal palace. Pope Sixtus IV added to what Nicholas had begun, providing the library with a suite of beautifully frescoed rooms and furnishing it with heavy wooden benches, to which the precious works were actually chained. But, most significantly, like the popes who

The Scripture quotations contained herein are from the New Revised Standard Version Bible,
copyright © 1989 by the Division of Christian Education of the National Council of the
Churches of Christ in the U.S.A., and are used by permission.
All rights reserved.

The illustrations in this book are taken from Latin volumes in the collections of The Vatican
Library, including the Barberini, Capponi, Chigi, Borghese, Ottoboni, Reginense, Urbino
and Rossiano collections. The sources for each illustration appear on page 80.

Published by Turner Publishing, Inc.
A Subsidiary of Turner Broadcasting System, Inc.
1050 Techwood Drive, N.W.
Atlanta, Georgia 30318

First Edition 10 9 8 7 6 5 4 3 2 1

Library of Congress Cataloging-in-Publication Data
Take up my cross . . . —1st ed.
p. cm. —(Treasures of the Vatican Library)
Contains illustrations from various Vatican Library manuscripts with each illustration
accompanied by a Bible scripture from the New Revised Standard Version Bible.
ISBN 1-57036-235-1 (alk. paper)
1. Jesus Christ—Crucifixion—Art. 2. Illumination of books and manuscripts, Medieval.
3. Illumination of books and manuscripts—Vatican City. 4. Biblioteca apostolica vaticana.
I. Biblioteca apostolica vaticana. II. Turner Publishing, Inc.
III. Bible. English. New Revised Standard. Selections. 1995. IV. Series.
ND3338.T35 1995
745.6'7'0940902—dc20 95-169
CIP

Printed in Hong Kong.

Treasures of The Vatican Library
(Book Illustration, Volume 5)

Take Up
My Cross...

Turner Publishing, Inc.

ATLANTA

Take Up
My Cross...